2/2012

Treachery and Betrayal
at Jolly Days

Don't miss the first spine-tingling
Secrets of Dripping Fang adventure!

SECRETS OF
DRIPPING FANG
BOOK ONE:
The Onts

SECRETS OF

DRIPPING FANG

BOOK TWO

Treachery and Betrayal at Jolly Days

DAN GREENBURG

Illustrations by SCOTT M. FISCHER

HARCOURT, INC.

Orlando   Austin   New York   San Diego   Toronto   London

*I want to thank my editor, Allyn Johnston, for her macabre yet soulful
sense of humor, for her eagerness to explore ideas beyond the bounds of taste,
for understanding an author's poignant thirst for praise, and for helping
me say exactly what I'm trying to say, except more gooder.
I also want to thank Scott M. Fischer,
an artist with dizzying technical abilities and a demented genius
at combining terror and humor in the same illustration.*
—D. G.

www.HarcourtBooks.com

Illustrations copyright © 2006 by Scott M. Fischer

Library of Congress Cataloging-in-Publication Data
Greenburg, Dan.
Secrets of Dripping Fang. Book two, Treachery and betrayal
at Jolly Days/Dan Greenburg; [illustrated by Scott M. Fischer].
p. cm.
Summary: The ten-year-old Shluffmuffin twins,
still evading the evil, giant ants that tried to adopt them,
discover the culinary delights of swamps and encounter a zombie
who bears a strange resemblance to their deceased father.
[1. Orphans—Fiction. 2. Twins—Fiction. 3. Brothers
and sisters—Fiction. 4. Swamps—Fiction. 5. Ants—Fiction.
6. Zombies—Fiction. 7. Cincinnati (Ohio)—Fiction.]
I. Fischer, Scott M., ill. II. Title.
PZ7.G8278Sec 2006
[Fic]—dc22 2005001941
ISBN-13: 978-0-15-205463-2 ISBN-10: 0-15-205463-4

Text set in Meridien
Designed by Linda Lockowitz

First edition
A C E G H F D B

Printed in the United States of America

For Judith and Zack
with spooky love
—D. G.

Contents

Treachery and Betrayal
at Jolly Days

CHAPTER 1

Hitching to Cincinnati with a Guy Named Verne

After the gloom of Dripping Fang Forest, the blue white light from the full moon was almost blinding. Cheyenne and Wally emerged from the trees and found themselves out on the highway. The sky in the east was only just beginning to lighten up at the edges. There was no traffic, but they could see a lone car approaching in the distance.

"You think it's safe to hitchhike?" Wally asked.

"Sure," said Cheyenne. "What could possibly happen to us hitchhiking?"

"I don't know," said Wally, "but in the past twenty-four hours, we were adopted by two ladies who turned out to be giant ants, we were attacked by a glowing ten-foot-long slug, we nearly had our throats torn out by man-eating wolves, and a really nice professor who invited us to tea turned out to have a wife who's an enormous eight-legged spider. And you're asking what could happen to us *hitchhiking*?"

Although Wally and Cheyenne Shluffmuffin were twins, their outlooks on life were quite different. Cheyenne saw only the good side of life, Wally only the bad. Cheyenne saw a beach and thought hot sand and thundering surf. Wally saw a beach and thought sunstroke, riptides, and choking on salt water.

As the car approached, the twins stuck out their thumbs. They heard the high hum of the car's tires go down the scale as it slowed up, then heard the car *yerp* to a stop.

"Hi there!" called the driver, a man with a gray crew cut. "You kids like a lift?"

"Yes, if you're going toward Cincinnati," asked Wally.

"Sure am," said the driver. "Hop in."

Wally climbed inside. Cheyenne got in after him and slammed the door. The car took off again.

"Name's Verne," said the driver. "What they call *you*?"

"I'm Cheyenne, he's Wally," said Cheyenne.

"You kids look pretty young to be out so late, all alone on a deserted highway," said Verne. "Your mommy and daddy know you're out so late?"

"Our mommy and daddy are dead," said Wally.

"Oh, sorry to hear that," said Verne. "Who's been takin' care of you?"

"Hortense Jolly and two giant ants," said Wally.

"That's okay, you don't have to tell me if you don't want to," said Verne. "I was just makin' conversation. Me, I used to work at Wright-Patterson Air Force Base. I was a janitor in Hangar 18, where they did autopsies on the aliens they found in them UFO crashes."

"Really?" said Cheyenne. She stifled a sneeze.

4

"Yep. I swiped me a alien brain once as a souvenir. Put 'er in a jar of alcohol, figured she might be worth somethin' someday. Keep 'er in my trunk, if you wanna have a peek." He winked at them. "Whattaya say, wanna take a peek at 'er?"

"No thanks," said Wally. "We wouldn't want to slow you down."

"It wouldn't slow me down none," said Verne. "It wouldn't take no time at all. I could just pull over to the shoulder and pop the trunk."

"Maybe some other time," said Wally. "We're in kind of a hurry to get back to Cincinnati."

"Fair enough," said Verne, "fair enough. We'll do it some other time, then. You just tell me when."

Wally leaned close to Cheyenne and whispered in her ear: "This guy's a weirdo. First time he stops, we're making a run for it."

Cheyenne nodded. Approaching them, way in the distance, were the headlights of a very large truck. She dreamily watched them getting larger and larger.

"What type of music you kids like to listen to while we drive?" Verne asked.

"Oh, happy songs," said Cheyenne, blotting her runny nose.

"Happy songs, eh? Okay, let's see what we got here," said Verne.

He leaned across the twins, opened the glove compartment, and started to rummage through it.

"Maybe you should keep your eyes on the road, Verne," said Wally.

"Good advice, buddy," said Verne, still rummaging. "Darned good advice."

The truck, an eighteen-wheeler, hurtled toward them in the opposite lane. As Verne's car drifted over the double yellow line into its path, the truck driver flashed his brights and sounded his air horn. Verne kept on rummaging.

Just before the vehicles collided in an ugly mangle of metal, Wally grabbed the steering wheel and yanked it hard to the right. The truck swerved. The car rocked violently in the whoosh of air from the passing truck. Wally yanked the wheel back to the left before they hit the shoulder.

"Whoo-hoo!" yelled Verne. "Close one! The way these truckers drive, it's a wonder they give 'em licenses at *all*, eh, Wally?"

"Yeah," Wally gasped.

"Well, little lady," said Verne to Cheyenne, "all I could find is this here CD of *Greatest Funeral Favorites,* if that's okay with you."

"That's fine." Cheyenne gulped.

So they listened in silence to an hour of suffocatingly grim organ music from *Greatest Funeral Favorites* as they drove to Cincinnati while the sky turned pink in the east.

The first stoplight they hit was a five-way intersection that bordered the swamps at the city limits. Cheyenne and Wally leaped out of the car and ran for their lives.

CHAPTER 2

Enter the Zombie

In the Cincinnati swamps lived alligators whose jaws could crush their victims like a soda can but whose brains were the size of a Tootsie Roll. Also in the swamps lived many types of mosquitoes, dragonflies, frogs, toads, ticks, turtles, lizards, leeches, worms, grubs, caterpillars, centipedes, chiggers, snakes, snails, spiders, slugs, and some creatures so covered with slime, so gross and disgusting, that nobody, not even the scientists who studied them, knew or cared what they were.

But as gross and disgusting as these creatures were, they were absolutely *adorable* compared with the one that now painfully dragged itself over the spongy ground. This creature was a zombie, a member of the living dead. Much of the rotting skin that had once been his face still clung to his skull. But much of the rest of it had dropped off and been swallowed up by the swamps.

The zombie had been singing a song: "Itsy bitsy spider climbed up the waterspout," but through his rotting teeth and lips, it sounded more like: "Issy bissy spy clyde uppa waaa spow."

As the Shluffmuffin twins raced past on the deserted road that bordered the swamps, the zombie paused and looked in their direction. He saw that the sky was pink and that the sun was about to come up, gold and horrible, at any moment. He would have to quickly crawl back into his cave to wait out the day.

Still humming "Issy bissy spy clyde uppa waaa spow," the zombie dragged himself off toward his cave. Something fell into a puddle with a little plopping sound. He fished it out and studied it closely. It looked kind of familiar. It *was* familiar. It was his left ear. With a bitter laugh, he tossed it into the swamps.

CHAPTER 3

Jolly Days, We're Here Again

The sun popped over the horizon, flooding the street with yellow. Squinting in the glare, Wally and Cheyenne hurried past a row of red brick buildings, with steep stone stairways, to the one that housed the Jolly Days Orphanage. The steps of Jolly Days had more cracks than those of their neighbors, and some were frighteningly loose. But they'd been scrubbed so clean by orphans, you could lick them without getting sick, assuming you were somebody who licked steps. Wally knocked on the front door.

A moment later the door creaked inward, and there stood Hortense Jolly, trying to act excited to see them. "Cheyenne! Wally! How

11

marvelous to see you! It seems like only yesterday that you two were residents here."

"It *was* only yesterday that we were residents here," said Wally. "That's when we left."

"Yes, well, I meant that it seemed a lot longer," she said. "Like the day *before* yesterday at the very least. Well, do come in, come in. The children are dying to see you and hear what you've been up to. Would you do me a tremendous favor, though? Don't tell them about anything that was the least bit, you know . . ."

"Sickening? Revolting? Sure to make them puke?" Wally suggested.

"Exactly. I wouldn't want them to worry that getting adopted might, you know . . ."

"Get them killed?" Wally suggested.

"I knew you'd understand, dear," said Hortense, giving his cheek a squeeze.

The twins were oddly glad to be back. They inhaled the familiar smell of the orphanage, a combination of strong hospital soap and rotting rat carcasses. They realized they were happy to see their fellow orphans—even Rocco, the bully who had tried to pin nasty nicknames on them like Sniffles and Stinkfoot.

Miss Jolly shepherded the twins into the dining room and bonged the heavy brass bell with a soup ladle.

"Attention, orphans of Jolly Days! Our old friends the Shluffmuffin twins have come back to pay us a visit. Sadly, their trial adoption has hit a little snag, so they've asked to return to Jolly Days while we work it out. Let us all stand now and sing our 'Song for Orphans Whose Adoption Has Hit a Snag.'"

The orphans stood up at their places at the breakfast table and sang another of the songs that Hortense Jolly, who planned someday to write musicals for Broadway, had composed for them:

"So you screwed up your adoption, what a mess!
Will Miss Jolly take you back at this address?
If she does, do not refuse her,
You pathetic little loser.
We never thought you'd make it, we confess.

"So you didn't get new parents, and that sucks.
And you're still a lonely orphan kid—aww
     shucks!
But the worst part of the deal,
You unfortunate schlemiel,
Is Miss Jolly's out at least six hundred bucks."

Then they all sat down to a breakfast of stale bread crusts and a thin gray soup called gruel that looked like mucus.

"So, Sniffles and Stinkfoot, how did you screw it up?" asked Rocco.

Wally couldn't believe the big fat bully was trying to pin unpleasant nicknames on them again. He walked over to Rocco and matter-of-factly punched him in the stomach.

"We didn't screw it up," said Cheyenne, loudly blowing her nose into a Kleenex.

"Then why'd you come back?" asked a boy named Orville.

The twins looked at Hortense. She flashed them a strained smile.

"We had ... a disagreement with the ladies who were thinking of adopting us," Wally answered.

"What kind of disagreement?" asked a girl named Florrie.

"Well," said Cheyenne, "we just wanted a normal home life with a couple of nice parents, and they ..."

"... wanted to breed a race of super-ants to enslave the human race and end life on Earth as we know it," said Wally.

Hortense winced and shook her head. The orphans began chattering excitedly.

"Wally, I thought we had an agreement," Hortense said.

"I'm sorry, Miss Jolly," said Wally. "I just can't pretend that the Mandible sisters were normal adopters. They weren't. They were giant ants."

"That's *enough*, Wally!" snapped Hortense. "All right, you have just won yourself the privilege of cleaning all the toilets in the orphanage

16

today, young man. And after that, you will scrape all the gum off the bottom of the dining room table."

"Who cares?" said Wally. "I've done both of those things so much, I don't even mind them anymore. In fact, I kind of like them."

"In that case," said Hortense, "you will not be permitted to either clean the toilets *or* scrape the gum."

"Aww," said Wally. "Can't I just scrape the gum?"

The orphans giggled. Hortense glared at Wally, but he didn't turn away.

As soon as breakfast was over, the orphans clustered around the Shluffmuffin twins and pumped them about their adventures. When the kids heard about the Onts' plan to kill the twins, their narrow escape from Mandible House, the attack of the giant slug, their escapes from the man-eating wolves and the enormous spider, they were jealous.

"That is so cool," said Orville. "Nothing that cool ever happens to *us*."

"I wish *I* could do some of those cool things," said Florrie.

"Yeah, I've never even *seen* a giant slug," said Ellie Mae.

"How did you get away from the giant slug?" asked Rocco.

"I poured salt on him," said Cheyenne.

"Why didn't you just blow your nose on him?" said Rocco.

"What did you say, Piggy?" asked Wally.

"I said why didn't you shove your stinky feet in the slug's face so the fumes would poison his lungs?"

Wally sighed, got up, walked slowly over to Rocco, and punched him in the stomach again.

"That didn't even hurt," said Rocco.

Wally punched him with all his might.

"*That* did," Rocco wheezed.

Later, while the orphans were busy doing their chores, Hortense furtively slipped away to

her bedroom. Glancing nervously over her shoulder, she looked up a phone number in her address book. She picked up the phone and, with shaking forefinger, dialed the number.

The phone rang three times and somebody answered on the other end.

"Mandible House," said a familiar voice.

CHAPTER 4

Treachery, Betrayal, Double and Triple Crosses

"Is this Miss Mandible?" whispered Hortense.

"What?" said the voice. "Speak up, I can't hear you."

"I said, is this Miss Mandible?" asked Hortense a little louder.

"Who wants to know, and why the devil are you whispering?" asked Dagmar.

"It's me, Hortense Jolly. From the Jolly Days Orphanage?" said Hortense a little louder yet. "I understand there's a problem with the Shluffmuffin twins."

"Who told you there was a problem?" asked Dagmar.

"Well, Wally and Cheyenne did," whispered

Hortense. "They just came back here this morning."

"If you don't speak louder, I'm hanging up this phone right now," said Dagmar.

"I said, *Wally and Cheyenne told me there was a problem, Miss Mandible! They just came back here this morning!*" shouted Hortense into the phone.

"You say the twins have returned to the orphanage?" asked Dagmar.

"Yes," said Hortense.

"And they are there now?"

"Yes."

"Thank you, Ms. Jolly. My sister and I will be there as quickly as we can."

"Good."

Hortense hung up the phone and realized that Wally and Cheyenne were standing in the doorway, staring at her. It suddenly felt about twenty degrees too warm in the room. It felt as though there wasn't enough air for three people to breathe.

"Uh, hi there," said Hortense.

"How could you do that, Miss Jolly?" Wally

demanded. "How could you sell us out like that?"

"We trusted you, Miss Jolly," said Cheyenne. "How could you betray us?"

"Well, uh, I didn't betray you, dears. Oh no, I'd never betray you. I just—"

"What do you *mean* you'd never betray us?" Wally demanded. "We *heard* you. We heard you say, 'Wally and Cheyenne told me there was a problem, Miss Mandible! They just came back here this morning!'"

"Oh, that. Well, that just kind of . . . slipped out," said Hortense. "I'm so sorry, children."

"You're *sorry*?" said Wally. "Giant ant-women are coming here to kill us, and you're *sorry*?"

"Oh, I hardly think they're coming here to kill you."

"So you do admit they're coming here?"

"Well, yes. But not to *kill* you, dear, to take you back *home* with them. To take you back home and—"

"—and *kill* us, Miss Jolly," said Wally. "Because I saw the hundreds of super-larvae they're breeding in their basement, and because we found out they're planning to take over Earth and enslave the human race."

"What makes you think they're planning to enslave the human race?"

"They admitted it, Miss Jolly," said Cheyenne.

"They did? Honest and truly? Cross your heart and hope to die?"

"Yes!"

"Hmm. Well, that puts a different light on the matter, doesn't it?" Hortense thought this over. "I don't suppose you'd be willing to go back home with them for just a *teensy* while so that we can earn our six-hundred-dollar adoption fee?"

Wally and Cheyenne glared at her.

"All right, all right, perhaps that isn't such a good idea. Well then, what do you suggest we do?"

"We need to protect ourselves," said Cheyenne. "We need to get out of here before they come."

"I'll pack you some lunch," said Hortense. "Come with me."

She led them into the kitchen and put some food into a brown paper bag.

"Where will you go?" Hortense asked.

"We don't know," said Wally.

"Why don't you children stay here at the orphanage? I can hide you while the Mandible sisters are here—the downstairs broom closet is a perfect place. And when they leave I can take care of you."

"I don't know," said Wally.

"I think Miss Jolly is right," said Cheyenne. "There's really nowhere else we can go. She may be greedy, stingy, cheap, disloyal, and mean, but I don't think Miss Jolly'd ever try to eat us."

"I guess you're right," said Wally.

"Then you'll stay at Jolly Days?" asked Hortense.

"I guess so," said Wally. "I hope we're not making a big mistake."

CHAPTER 5

Longing for the Patter of Tiny Feet Around the House—Hundreds of Tiny Feet Around the House

"You know who I miss?" said Shirley Spydelle, the enormous eight-legged spider. "Those wonderful little children, Wally and Cheyenne."

She lay back in the middle of the huge web she had just spun across the living room and checked it for broken strands.

Edgar, her human husband, settled in the hammock he had set up alongside the web. He lit a match and touched it to his pipe.

"But did you actually *meet* Wally and Cheyenne, my love?" Edgar asked in his adorable British accent, sucking at the flame.

"They unfortunately left before we were introduced," Shirley admitted. "But are you saying that just because I never met them I can't miss them?"

"Not exactly, dear, but most people do tend to miss only the people they've met."

"Well, I'm not most people, Edgar, am I?"

Edgar's pipe went out. He lit another match and sucked the flame into the bowl again.

"No, dear," said Edgar, "you're certainly not. Oh, my word, there's a rip in your web. Right over there. See where I'm pointing?"

"Right. Thanks, love," said Shirley.

She squeezed out a thin line of liquid from the spinnerets under her abdomen. It immediately dried and became a silky thread. She used the thread to replace the torn section of her web.

"You know, Edgar, just having those dear

28

children in our home for even that brief time has reawakened powerful longings in me. Powerful longings to have children of our own."

"But if we had children of our own, dear, you'd have to eat me after we mated. I mean, that's what spiders do, isn't it? We've discussed this many times."

Shirley sighed. "I know, Edgar, I know. But I would *so* love to have a ton of kids crawling all over the place."

"Well, then, why don't we adopt?"

"Adopt? Hmm. You know, Edgar, that's not such a bad idea. Not such a bad little idea at all. And if we adopted, I probably wouldn't have to eat you."

Edgar got out the Yellow Pages. Under *Adoptions, Human,* he found three listings: Kids 'n' Stuff, Adoptions "Я" Us, and Jolly Days Orphanage of Cincinnati. Both he and Shirley were most impressed by the full-page ad for the Jolly Days Orphanage:

Edgar picked up the phone and made an appointment for the following Monday.

CHAPTER 6

The Return
of the Giant Adopters

By the time the doorbell rang, Hortense Jolly had become so frightened at the thought of the Mandible sisters, she almost couldn't move. Wally and Cheyenne had finally convinced her that they *were* giant ants, and the thought of that made her shudder. She couldn't even stand the sight of ants at a picnic.

The doorbell rang again. It gave Hortense a prickly feeling on her scalp, and between her shoulder blades, and all the way down her spine.

Her first idea was not to answer the bell, pretend that no one was home or that everyone was in the bathroom. But the Mandibles would never buy that. Thirty-eight orphans lived there, too. They couldn't all be in the bathroom at once.

Her second idea was to tell the Mandibles an outright lie: "This'll make you giggle. I *thought* it was Wally and Cheyenne who came back, but I was wrong. See, I'm very nearsighted and I wasn't wearing my glasses, so when I called you and said . . ."

Her third idea was to just act tough with them: "Listen, you stupid ants, you think you can take over the human race and end life on Earth as we know it? Well, I'm not taking any crap from you, see? You give me a hard time, I'll *step* on you. I've stepped on far better ants than you in my time, believe me."

Her fourth idea was to simply throw herself on their mercy: "Please! Have mercy on me! I'll do anything you say, *anything*! Just don't hurt me! *Please!*"

The ringing of the doorbell grew more persistent. Now there was a pounding on the door as well. If they kept that up, they could break it down. It would cost a couple hundred dollars to replace.

So Hortense went to the door and opened it. The Mandible sisters stood in the doorway, looming over her, looking bigger and scarier than she remembered in their huge black sunglasses and their huge black hats and their long black gloves.

"Well, hello there!" said Hortense, trying to sound more jolly than tense. "So good to see you again! Come in, come in!"

"We've brought the signed adoption documents," said Dagmar, handing her a sheaf of papers.

"Good-good-good!"

"And a check for the adoption," said Dagmar, handing it to her. "We trust you will find it to your liking."

"Ah yes, the six hundred dollars," said Hortense, looking at the check. "Good, I'm glad that you remembered to . . . that you remembered to . . ."

Hortense looked at the check again. It didn't

say six hundred dollars. It said *nine* hundred dollars!

"Nine hundred dollars?" Hortense squeaked.

"We've added a bonus of three hundred dollars for being so helpful and for finding us exactly what we were looking for," Hedy explained.

Nine hundred dollars! The thought of that much money made Hortense absolutely dizzy with pleasure. True, she wouldn't be able to keep it all. True, she had generously—perhaps *too* generously—promised the orphans she'd always share her profits by giving each of them a shiny new penny every time an orphan was adopted.

But with Wally and Cheyenne gone, that would be only thirty-six new pennies she had to cough up. What was nine hundred dollars, minus thirty-six cents? Eight hundred ninety-nine dollars and sixty-four cents! Okay, that wasn't bad at all.

"You find the amount of the check acceptable?" Dagmar asked.

"Oh yes, yes," said Hortense. "Quite acceptable."

"Excellent," said Dagmar. "And now, where are the Shluffmuffins?"

"Um, oh, the Shluffmuffins," said Hortense.

"Yes, the Shluffmuffins," said Dagmar.

Hortense had temporarily lost her mind, thinking about all that money. Now she had to deal with the fact that the Mandible sisters expected to get what they paid for. *And* the fact that she had promised to hide the twins in the broom closet and keep them safe.

"Well," said Hortense, "they're around here *somewhere*. I'll have to go and look."

She started to leave, but Dagmar caught her by the wrist.

"You're quite sure they're here?" Dagmar asked.

"Oh yes, quite sure," said Hortense. "Well, *fairly* sure, anyway. You never know for certain with kids, though. Ha-ha. One moment they're here, and the next . . . I'll just go and have a look around to see—"

Dagmar took Hortense's pinkie finger and bent it backward ever so slightly. "I do hope you aren't having any doubts about turning over the twins to us," she said in her steely voice. "You aren't, are you?"

Hortense's eyes got very wide.

Dagmar bent the pinkie finger back a little farther, just enough to make Hortense squeak again, but not from pleasure.

"Any doubts at all, Hortense?"

"No doubts," gasped Hortense.

"Excellent," said Dagmar. "And where is it that they're hiding?" She bent the pinkie finger back even farther.

"Broom closet," gasped Hortense.

"The broom closet," said Dagmar. "Excellent. Since my sister and I aren't familiar with the layout here, why don't you just take us to the broom closet now?"

Hortense nodded rapidly. Then, with her pinkie finger still trapped, she led the Mandibles down the hall. She felt bad about betraying Wally and Cheyenne, but she felt even worse about her painfully bent-back pinkie finger.

When they arrived at the broom closet, Hortense stopped.

"Is this where the children are hiding, dear?" asked Hedy.

Hortense nodded.

"Wonderful, dear," said Hedy. "Thank you so much."

Dagmar let go of Hortense's pinkie finger and flung open the door.

The broom closet was empty.

"What th—?" Hedy sputtered.

"Where are the Shluffmuffins?" Dagmar demanded.

"I . . . I don't know," said Hortense. "I really don't know."

"You don't *know*?" Dagmar was furious. "What do you *mean* you don't know?"

"I just don't," said Hortense. "I really thought they were in the broom closet."

"BUT YOU TOLD US THIS WAS WHERE THEY WERE! YOU TOLD US YOU HAD NO DOUBTS ABOUT TURNING THE TWINS OVER TO US! ISN'T THAT WHAT YOU TOLD US?"

"Y-yes," said Hortense nervously. "Th-that's what I told, and that's what I believed. You can break off my finger, but I still won't know where they are. I put them in the broom closet and told them to hide there, and now they're gone!"

"Find them! Search the building!" said Dagmar. "Hedy, you take the first floor! I'll take the second!"

Dagmar ran upstairs. Orphans looked up from their scouring and polishing.

"Where are the Shluffmuffins?" Dagmar demanded. "Have you seen them?"

"Where are the *who*?" asked Rocco.

"The Shluffmuffins, you idiot!" said Dagmar.

"Don't know anyone by that name," said Rocco. He turned to the others. "You know anyone named Stuffmuffin?"

"Not *Stuff*muffin, *Shluff*muffin!" Dagmar corrected.

"We once had a kid named Sluppmurfin," said Orville, "but he ain't here no more. I think he got himself adopted."

The orphans giggled.

"I used to know a boy named Slop Murphy," said Florrie, "but he died."

The orphans howled with laughter.

Dagmar could scarcely contain her anger.

"You do not know whom you're dealing with here," she said in a voice that was hollow and echoey. "You may *think* you know, but you do not have the slightest idea."

"Oooooo, are we supposed to be afraid now?" asked Rocco.

"Be afraid or don't be afraid," said Dagmar in her echoey voice. "It doesn't matter. But neither choice will make you safe."

As Dagmar passed a window, something on the street below caught her eye: two figures scampering down the front steps of the orphanage. The Shluffmuffins!

"Hedy!" Dagmar shouted. "It's the twins! They're escaping!"

CHAPTER 7

A Big Bad Bus Ride to Nowhere

Just as Wally and Cheyenne climbed aboard the big green crosstown bus, they saw Hedy and Dagmar burst out of the orphanage. The Onts came racing toward them, shouting and waving their many arms.

"Driver, please close the doors!" yelled Wally.

In reply, the bus driver pointed to the coin box.

A sign above his head said EXACT CHANGE RE-QUIRED. IT HAPPENS TO BE THE LAW. Wally and Cheyenne had won a little money from the other orphans, betting on cockroach races. Luckily, Wally had it with him. He dropped several coins in the coin box.

"Wait! Wait!" shouted Dagmar and Hedy, their arms flailing like ostriches trying to take flight. "Wait for us!"

"Please close the doors, sir!" cried Cheyenne.

"Just as soon as we pick up those two ladies," said the driver.

"They aren't ladies, sir!" said Wally. "They're giant ants!"

"They're what?" said the driver. He seemed annoyed.

"Giant ants!" said Wally. "Evil giant ants in human clothes! You don't want them on your bus, believe me!"

The driver frowned at the twins. His already creased face bunched up around his eyes and forehead.

Dagmar and Hedy were almost up to the bus now.

"They're really dangerous," Cheyenne pleaded. "I know it sounds crazy, but they're killers! They're planning to take over the human race!"

"And they never have exact change!" Wally added in desperation.

"They *what*?" said the driver.

"They never have exact change," said Wally. "They don't believe in it."

"*Nobody* gets on this bus without exact change," said the driver angrily. "It happens to be the law!" He closed the doors with a great *whoosh*, just as the Onts rushed up.

"Open your doors!" Dagmar shouted. "Open your doors immediately!"

"No way!" yelled the driver.

"You do not know whom you're dealing with here!" shouted Dagmar.

"I sure do!" shouted the driver. "You people think I got nothing better to do all day than break bills and make change? Do all that math in my head? Well, I got big news for you, lady! I happen to be a *bus driver*, not a *banker*!"

The driver was breathing hard now. His face was a pink balloon about to burst. Flecks of foam had formed in the corners of his mouth.

"This used to be a great country!" he screamed. "A beautiful country, with . . . with spacious skies and amber waves of grain! With . . . with purple mountains majesties above the fruited plain! *You people that never have exact change have ruined it for the rest of us!*"

Dagmar struck the folding doors with one of her four fists. Cracks spider-webbed across the glass and shattered it. Glass splinters plinked to the floor of the bus.

The driver stamped on the gas pedal. The bus tore away from the curb.

As the Mandible sisters shrank in the distance, Wally and Cheyenne saw them flag down a cab and get inside. A moment later the cab surged forward, and soon it caught up with the bus.

"What are we going to do?" asked Cheyenne. "They're going to follow us to the end of the line, and then they're going to grab us."

Wally looked around. The bus had left most of the city behind. There were no buildings in sight. On the right side were nothing but empty fields with scrubby bushes and empty lots stacked with rubbish and old tires. On the left side were the swamps.

The traffic signal swinging from an overhead wire turned red. The driver pulled up to it and stopped.

"Driver, we're getting off here," said Wally.

"We're almost at the end of the line," said the driver. "You have to wait till then."

"We can't wait till then," said Wally. "We have to get off here."

"Look around you," said the driver. "There's no *here* here."

"We have to get off, though," said Wally.

"Suit yourself," said the driver in a grumpy voice. "What do *I* care?"

The doors with the shattered glass whooshed open.

Wally grabbed his sister's hand. Together they jumped off the bus and raced across the road toward the swamps.

"Is this a good idea?" asked Cheyenne as they ran.

"Our only chance is to lose them in the swamps," said Wally.

They heard the Onts' cab screech to a stop behind the bus. They saw Dagmar and Hedy climb out of the cab, tear across the road, and head off after them.

CHAPTER 8

How to Drown in
Three Feet of Water

Amazingly, Wally and Cheyenne still carried the brown paper bag filled with food that Hortense Jolly had generously packed for them: stale bread crusts and a Snapple bottle filled with gruel and green floaty things that looked like boogers.

The swamps smelled like rotting eggs and had more mosquitoes than the twins thought existed. The kids smacked mosquitoes on their sweating necks and foreheads.

With each step Wally and Cheyenne took, their feet sank into the mushy ground. When they pulled them out again, their feet made loud sucking noises. It was like running underwater.

It was like running underwater with concrete sneakers.

The Onts had now entered the swamps as well. Looking back over their shoulders, the twins could catch glimpses of them, wide-brimmed black hats bobbing up and down as they ran.

Cheyenne and Wally slogged along for half an hour before they stopped to rest.

"I don't hear them anymore," said Cheyenne. "I think we lost them."

"Ants are guided by smells," said Wally, who'd had to memorize all the A-words in the encyclopedia during his stay at Jolly Days. (Every orphan had been assigned a letter to memorize—that was Hortense Jolly's substitute for schooling.) "And since everybody says my feet stink worse than barn animals," Wally continued, "they're sure to find us sooner or later."

"What do you think will happen if they catch us?" she asked.

"If we're lucky," said Wally, "they'll kill us quickly."

49

"Oh," said Cheyenne. "Well then, I hope we're lucky. I guess."

She sat down beside a half-submerged log and unlaced a soggy sneaker.

There was something odd about that log. As Wally tried to figure out what it was, he saw two bumps on the log become eyes. Immediately he flung himself onto the log, wrapping his arms around its nearest end.

"Run, Cheyenne, run!" Wally shouted.

The log came suddenly alive—splashing, thrashing, twisting, rolling over and over and over and over in the shallow water. An alligator! Wally gamely hung on to the alligator's head, his arms clamping the huge mouth shut.

As soon as Cheyenne had scrambled away, Wally let go and threw himself clear of the now snapping jaws.

"Well, thanks for saving my life," said Cheyenne when she was once more able to speak. "But how did you ever manage to hold its jaws closed?"

"*Alligator* was one of the encyclopedia words

I had to memorize," said Wally. "So I knew that gators can snap their jaws shut with a pressure of three thousand pounds per square inch, but they've got practically no strength to open them. You can just about hold a gator's jaws closed with one hand."

"Am I ever grateful you learned your *A*s!" said Cheyenne. "Hey, do you smell something?"

"Yeah," he said. "I smell *us*. We smell like we've been rolling in rotten omelets."

"I don't mean that," she said. "I mean do you smell chocolate?"

"Chocolate? You're crazy. Why would there be chocolate in a swamp?" Wally took a deep breath. "No, wait. You're right. I *do* smell it. It *is* chocolate. Yumm. I'm so hungry, I'd eat a *snake* if it was dipped in chocolate."

"It's coming from over there," said Cheyenne, pointing to a curtain of leaves and vines hanging from the branch of a tree.

They slogged through the mud toward the curtain of leaves and vines. That's when Wally began sinking into the swamp up to his knees.

"Uh-oh," said Wally. "This better not be what I think it is."

"What do you think it is?" asked Cheyenne nervously, sinking up to her thighs.

"Quicksand," said Wally, sinking up to his waist. "Okay, here's the deal about quicksand. If you struggle, you'll get sucked below the surface, you'll choke and drown and die a horrible death. But if you just relax, you'll float and you'll be fine."

"I'm sinking!" cried Cheyenne, flailing her arms, sinking up to her chest.

"That's because you're panicking!" yelled Wally. "Stop panicking, Cheyenne! Relax! Relax or die!"

"You can't scream 'Relax or die!' at somebody and expect them to relax!" shouted Cheyenne, sinking up to her shoulders. "I'm going to die!"

"You are not going to die, and I am not screaming," said Wally, switching to a very calm, very controlled voice. "I'm talking in a very calm, very controlled voice. See? And I'm not panicking. And I've stopped sinking. I'm floating now. See?"

Wally had, indeed, relaxed. He had leaned his head back, and the rest of his body had slowly bobbed back up to the surface. He was floating on his back, as if he were lying in a big tub of oatmeal instead of a deadly pool of quicksand.

"Think of something relaxing," said Wally. "Think of a beautiful palm-tree-lined beach with sparkling white sand and warm turquoise water."

Cheyenne tried to relax. She closed her eyes and tried to think nothing but calm thoughts as she sank up to her neck. She thought of a beautiful palm-tree-lined beach with sparkling white sand and warm turquoise water. She thought of a beautiful palm-tree-lined beach with sparkling turquoise sand and warm white water. And then, just as the quicksand reached her mouth, she felt her body bobbing back up to the surface.

"It's working," she said, amazed. "It's working! What do I do now?"

"Paddle slowly till you reach the shore," said Wally.

Both Wally and Cheyenne paddled very slowly, feet first, until they reached the edge of the pool of quicksand. When they at last touched solid ground, they slowly stood. Then they climbed up onto the bank.

"You saved me again," said Cheyenne. "How did you know about quicksand? It wasn't one of the *A*s."

"Yes it was," said Wally. *Avoiding Death by Quicksand.* Hey, there's that chocolate smell again."

"You're right," Cheyenne agreed. "And it's even stronger than before. It smells like . . . a huge pot of bubbling hot chocolate syrup. It seems to be coming from the other side of that curtain of leaves and vines . . ."

Being careful not to step into quicksand again, Cheyenne and Wally slogged toward the curtain of leaves and vines, and then they pushed on through it, eager to stuff their faces with rich brown gooey chocolate. Unfortunately, on the other side they saw not a huge pot of bubbling hot chocolate syrup but . . . two giant ants.

"Well, hello again, children," said Dagmar Mandible.

CHAPTER 9

Death by Chocolate

The Mandible sisters had taken off their long black gloves, their big black sunglasses, their big black hats, and their pink rubber human masks. They clearly didn't care anymore that Wally and Cheyenne could see them as they really looked, see their huge black claws, their horrible faces with their gigantic black eyes, the wavy antennae coming out of their foreheads, their horrible mouths that looked like huge pairs of horrible black pliers, only sharper.

Cheyenne gasped and covered her mouth to keep from screaming. Both twins shook with fear and stared at the Onts, bug-eyed. Neither Wally nor Cheyenne could speak a word.

"You're probably wondering where the chocolate is," said Dagmar. "Well, there isn't any. We just manufactured the smell of chocolate to make you come to us."

"Ants create smells as a way of talking to one another, my darlings," said Hedy. "We decided to talk to you through chocolate. Isn't that sweet?"

"Are you going to kill us now?" asked Wally in a shaky voice.

"Oh my, no, sweetheart," said Hedy. Then she looked at Dagmar. "We aren't, are we?"

"No, no," said Dagmar. "Not just now. Now we need to get some of your vital fluids and odors to feed the babies. The babies are *very* hungry."

Dagmar's horrible ant face softened a little as she thought of the hundreds of eyeless super-larvae in the Mandible House basement that would one day be big enough to climb out of their cocoons and replace humans as the rulers of Earth.

Cheyenne began sobbing silently.

Hedy reached a gigantic black claw into her

stylish Italian leather purse, took out a small package of Kleenex, and handed it to Cheyenne.

"Blow your nose, dear," she said.

Trying not to look at the claw, Cheyenne blew her nose. Hedy snatched the tissue out of Cheyenne's hands, stuck it in her purse, and handed her a fresh one.

"Blow your nose, dear," she said. "Blow it for the babies."

Shoulders shaking, Cheyenne blew again. And again. And again.

Hedy kept snatching snotty tissues out of her hands and replacing them with fresh ones.

Dagmar was busy wrapping plastic Baggies around Wally's feet to preserve their odor when she spotted the brown paper bag that Hortense had given them—and that, incredibly, had survived the ordeal in the quicksand.

"What's in the bag?" Dagmar asked.

That's when Cheyenne got her big idea.

"N-nothing," she said, pretending to hide the bag behind her back. "Just some junk you wouldn't be interested in."

"What kind of junk?" Dagmar asked.

Dagmar reached for the bag. Cheyenne clutched it to her chest.

"What have you got there?" Dagmar demanded. "What don't you want us to see?"

"Nothing!" screamed Cheyenne.

Dagmar tore at the brown paper bag with her claw, exposing the bottle of pale green liquid.

"What's in the bottle, darling?" asked Hedy.

"You want to know what's in the bottle?" repeated Cheyenne, her voice rising. "I'll *tell* you what's in the bottle. Something we stole from your basement! Something to feed your precious babies! A quart of snot we took right out of your Snot Press, that's what!"

"Give me that, you filthy thief!" shouted Dagmar.

"You want it?" screamed Cheyenne. "You really want it? Well then, *take* it!"

Cheyenne hurled the bottle of gruel as hard as she could at the quicksand. It landed in the middle of the pool with a soft *plop*. Dagmar lurched after the bottle like a dog after a Frisbee. The moment her feet hit the quicksand, she started to sink.

"What th—?" Dagmar cried as she sank up to her knees in the soft gooey liquid. "I'm sinking! What *is* this stuff?"

"Dagmar, darling," Hedy called, "are you all right?"

Her arms wildly windmilling, Dagmar sank up to her waist.

"Does it *look* like I'm all right, you idiot?" Dagmar snapped.

"What should I do, dear?" Hedy called.

"Pull me out of here before I drown, you imbecile!" Dagmar shouted, sinking up to her shoulders.

"Of course, of course," said Hedy. "But if I do that, darling, won't I drown, too?"

Cheyenne and Wally didn't hang around to hear Dagmar's answer. They took off in the opposite direction.

CHAPTER 10

At Least We Don't Have to Worry About Dagmar Anymore. Do We?

After twenty minutes of slow-motion slogging, the twins stopped for a rest.

"Well, I think we lost them," said Cheyenne.

"They've certainly got worse things to worry about now than chasing us," Wally agreed. "Hey, Cheyenne, that was pretty fast thinking with the Snapple bottle."

"Thanks," she said. "And now, we've seen the last of the Onts."

"I wouldn't be so sure of that," said Wally. He began looking for a sheltered space where they could spend the night.

"At least we don't have to worry about Dagmar anymore. She was sure sinking fast in that quicksand." Cheyenne wiped the perspiration off her forehead and slapped at a mosquito on her arm. "You know what I think?"

"What do you think?" said Wally.

"I think Dagmar was the only nasty one. I think that without Dagmar, Hedy wouldn't really be so bad."

"You know what *I* think?" said Wally.

"What?" said Cheyenne, slapping at a mosquito on her neck.

"I think you've got tapioca pudding for brains."

"Why?" said Cheyenne, slapping at a mosquito whining in her ear.

"Why? Because, just like Dagmar, Hedy is a giant ant who's breeding hundreds of super-larvae to take over Earth and enslave human beings. Hedy isn't Dagmar's *hostage*, Cheyenne. Dagmar wasn't holding a *gun* to Hedy's head. At no point did Hedy show she thought the whole idea of breeding super-larvae, taking over Earth,

63

enslaving human beings, or killing us to keep us quiet was anything but cool."

Cheyenne didn't answer, for three reasons: First, because when she thought about it, she knew that Wally had a point. Second, because she knew that neither of them had the slightest idea of how to get out of the swamps. Third, because she had become too busy slapping mosquitoes to talk.

The orange sun was sinking lower and lower in the west. It was getting bigger and oranger every minute. Not far away from where the Shluffmuffin twins searched for a sheltered place to spend the night, the zombie stirred. He was slowly awaking from his long day's sleep.

The zombie sat up, then lurched into a standing position. It was painful for him to stand after being asleep. With a little plopping sound, something fell into a puddle on the ground next to him. He bent over and fished it out. He studied it with great interest. It looked familiar. It was his other ear. He snorted and tossed it back into the puddle.

The sun, now blood-red, was ready to slip into the purple ground.

And, unfortunately for the twins, Dagmar was no longer sinking slowly in the quicksand. At her direction, Hedy had pushed over a rotten tree trunk until it fell across the pool of quicksand and, claw over claw, Dagmar was able to pull herself back along the trunk to safety.

"Dearest Dagmar," said Hedy happily, "I'm so terribly glad you're safe and sound. And," she added shyly, "I'm so proud I was able to save your precious life."

"Is that so?" asked Dagmar, brushing wet

sand off disgusting parts of her horrible ant body with her many claws. "I'm vastly amused to hear you think you had a significant role in saving me."

"Dagmar *darling*," said Hedy, shocked, her antennae drooping. "Surely you haven't forgotten who it was that pushed over the tree so you could pull yourself to safety? Surely you haven't forgotten *that*?"

"Surely you haven't forgotten who had to *tell* you to push over the tree?" said Dagmar. "Or who had to tell you exactly *how* to push it over, even though it was rotted clear through and could have been toppled by the breeze from the wings of a passing hummingbird?"

"Dagmar *sweetheart*," said Hedy, pouting. "Don't you recall how upset I was when you fell into the quicksand? I was positively *shattered*."

"What I recall," said Dagmar, "is screaming for you to pull me out of there. What I recall is your saying, 'But if I do that, darling, won't I drown, too?'"

"What good would it do you to have *both* of

us drown in quicksand?" cried Hedy. "To make orphans of our hundreds of precious ant babies? To have them die in snot-starved anguish, whimpering for human mucus? Is that what you wanted, Dagmar? Is it?"

Dagmar heaved a great ant sigh.

"No, Hedy, of course not," said Dagmar quietly. "We must never abandon the babies. We must never abandon our glorious and sacred mission to enslave humankind and end life on Earth as they know it."

She slid her left antennae through a claw, removing more moist grains of sand.

"I accept your apology," said Hedy.

"I don't recall offering one," said Dagmar, sliding her right antennae through the claw. "But that's not important now. The only important things now are recapturing those horrible Shluffmuffin twins. And harvesting more snot and foot odor. And preventing the twins from blabbing to other humans about our plans. And finding a punishment horrible enough to repay them for their treachery against us."

CHAPTER 11

Things You'd Be Willing to Eat If You Were Starving to Death in the Swamps

*F*our days later, Wally and Cheyenne were still lost in the steamy swamps on the outskirts of Cincinnati. Their clothes were soggy and stinky, and mold had begun to grow under their fingernails.

On the first day, they had eaten the last of the stale bread crusts that Hortense Jolly had packed for them. And although they hadn't thought much of it at the time, they now longed for the Snapple bottle full of gruel that Cheyenne had hurled into the quicksand.

On the second day, they tried eating leaves, grass, and flowers. Cheyenne said that leaves, grass, and flowers were healthy but didn't contain any protein, and they both needed to eat protein to live.

"So what contains protein?" asked Wally.

"Bugs," said Cheyenne.

"Bugs?" said Wally. "You expect me to eat *bugs*?"

"In lots of countries, bugs are delicacies," said Cheyenne. "Did you know that in Cambodia they eat fried spiders? And in Japan they eat fried wasps and grasshoppers?"

"Who told you that?"

"Nobody *told* me that, Wally. I learned that in the encyclopedia at Jolly Days. In Nigeria they eat roasted termites and caterpillars. In Thailand their favorites are dung beetles, stinkbugs, tarantulas, and giant water bugs."

"Did you know," said Wally, "some bugs are so poisonous that if you eat them, they cause paralysis or instant death?"

"Actually, I *did* know that," said Cheyenne.

They decided not to eat any bugs.

On the third day, though, they were even

hungrier. They were so hungry, they ate their first bug, a praying mantis. They also ate their first worm and their first caterpillar. Once they got past the absolute grossness, the squooshiness, the bitter taste, and the throwing up afterward, it wasn't so bad.

On the fourth day, they were hungrily turning over rocks and rotting logs and scraping bugs, grubs, worms, and caterpillars off the bottoms.

"You know what I think?" said Cheyenne.

"No, what?" said Wally.

"This isn't really too terrible, once you get used to it," said Cheyenne, biting into a centipede.

"You know what *I* think?" said Wally.

"What?"

"I think you've got moo shu pork for brains," said Wally. "Also, *I* was the one who found that centipede, so *I'm* the one who gets to eat it."

Wally grabbed the rest of the centipede out of Cheyenne's hands.

Suddenly, they heard a noise. A sort of creaking, groaning, splashing, slooshing, gurgling sound.

They looked up to see something that was even worse than eating centipedes. It was the zombie and he was dragging himself painfully in their direction. At the same moment they saw the zombie, he saw them, too. He began to wave and shout.

Screaming at the top of their lungs, the twins took off in the opposite direction.

The zombie stumbled after them, yelling, "Shy, Wa, me Da! Shy Wa, me Da!" But the sound of their screams made it impossible for them to hear what he was yelling.

Since the twins still had all their body parts and the zombie was rapidly losing his, Wally and Cheyenne ran faster. Soon they outdistanced him and disappeared. The zombie watched them go. He would have cried, but he had lost his tear ducts many months before.

CHAPTER 12

What's an Eight-Letter Word Beginning with P, Meaning "Someone Who's in Love with His Own Opinions"?

Police Lieutenant Ernie Kafka of the Cincinnati Metro Police Missing Persons Bureau stared down at the paper on his desk. He'd been staring at it so hard that the printed words blurred and he could hardly read what they said any longer. He chewed the end of a yellow wooden pencil and heard it crunch between his teeth. There had to be an answer here, there *had* to be, but what was it?

From out in the hallway came the sound of sobbing. There was a knock at the door. Kafka looked up.

"Come in!" called Kafka.

The desk sergeant, a man named Beckett, stuck his head in the door.

"Sorry to bother you, sir," said Beckett, "but I got a couple ladies here who—"

"Oh, thank heavens you're here, Beckett. What's a seven-letter word, beginning with *G*, meaning 'a type of dolphin that lives in the northern seas'?"

"*Grampus*, sir," said Beckett. "But I got a couple ladies here who—"

"*Grampus*," said Kafka. "Perfect!" He penciled the word into his *Cincinnati Enquirer* crossword puzzle. "Thank you, Beckett."

"You're welcome, sir," said Beckett. "Sir, I got a couple ladies here who want to file a missing persons report, but—"

"Okay, okay, hang on a second," said Kafka. "What's a nine-letter word beginning with *F*, meaning 'an awkwardly fat person'?"

"*Fustilugs*, sir," said the desk sergeant. "Sir, these ladies are kind of—"

"*Fustilugs*," said Kafka. "Of *course*! Thanks again, Beckett. Now what were you saying?"

"Sir, I got a couple ladies here who want to file a—"

"Wait wait wait! What's an eight-letter word beginning with *P,* meaning 'someone who's in love with his own opinions'?"

"*Philodox,* sir, but these ladies are—"

"*Philodox,*" said Kafka. "Yes! All right now, what were you saying, Sergeant?"

"Sir, I got a couple ladies out here who want to file a missing persons report, but they're so upset, I really need you to talk to them."

"Of course, Sergeant, of course," said Kafka. "Show them in."

Sergeant Beckett ushered two strange ladies into Lieutenant Kafka's office. They were both about six feet tall. They both wore large black sunglasses, large black hats, and elbow-length black gloves. One of them was sobbing loudly, and the other was patting her on the back and trying to comfort her.

"All right, ladies," said Kafka, "what seems to be the trouble here?"

"Sir, these are the Mandible sisters," said the

sergeant, "Hedy and Dagmar. It seems they adopted twin orphans, a boy and a girl, and the kids skipped out on them."

Kafka took out a clipboard and began filling out a missing persons report.

"Okay, what are the kids' names?" he asked.

"Walter and Cheyenne Shluffmuffin," said Hedy Mandible.

"Any identifying characteristics?"

"Both have red hair, freckles on their cheeks and noses, and identical salami-shaped birthmarks on their left shoulders," said Hedy. "The girl is always sneezing and blowing her nose. The boy's feet stink to high heaven."

"How old are they?" asked Kafka.

"They're only ten," said Dagmar Mandible between sobs. "We're so worried about them! Kids that age, all alone in Cincinnati—poor darlings! I shudder to think what could happen to them!"

"So they're runaways," said Kafka. "Any idea why they skipped out?"

"They didn't *skip* out, they ran," said Hedy.

"*Skip out* is a slang term for running away,"

said Beckett. "Do you know of any reason that they might have run away?"

"None," said Hedy. "We gave them everything, officers, *everything.* Each child had a separate room. Each child had an oak bed with several puffy pillows and a colorful quilt. Each—"

"Hang on a second," said Kafka, scribbling furiously. "I can't write that fast. Oak beds... puffy pillows... colorful quilts... Okay, what else?"

"Each child had an oak dresser with a mirror," said Hedy. "Each child had a color TV with extra cable channels, a laptop computer, and a PlayStation for video games."

"Holy mo!" said Kafka. "These kids don't know how good they had it. Tell you what. They don't come back, how's about me and the sergeant here come live with you instead?"

Hedy and Dagmar stared at Lieutenant Kafka.

"Are you and the sergeant orphans, dear?" asked Hedy.

"He was *kidding*, he was *kidding*," said Beckett. "Weren't you kidding, sir?"

"Yeah," said Kafka, "I was kidding. All right, ladies, is there anything else you want to add to this report?"

"Just one thing," said Dagmar.

"What?" asked Kafka.

"I'm embarrassed to tell you this," said Dagmar, "but, after all we gave them, these children stole from us."

"What did they steal from you, ma'am?" asked Kafka.

"Two laptop computers, two PlayStations for video games, and fifty pounds of expensive Belgian chocolates," said Dagmar.

CHAPTER 13

Pick Up a Quart of Milk, Dear, and a Few Nice Orphans

The Spydelles' van pulled up to the curb and parked beside the row of red brick buildings with steep stone stairways.

"Well, here we are, my dear," said Edgar. "The Jolly Days Orphanage. I feel sure this is where we'll find some lovely children to adopt."

He turned off the engine and pulled open the van's sliding door. "Want me to help you out onto the curb, darling, or can you do it yourself?"

"Why don't I just wait in the van?" said Shirley.

"Oh, I thought you wanted to come inside."

"I did, dear," said Shirley, "but now I think it might be best if I stay in the van. I don't want to alarm the children. You saw the effect I had on poor Wally and Cheyenne."

"Well, as we discussed, that was because Wally and Cheyenne had that unfortunate experience with those giant ants. *These* children haven't had such an experience."

"I know, but they might still be alarmed at the sight of an enormous spider entering the orphanage. Why don't you go and look over the orphans, and I'll just wait for you here."

"Whatever you say, my darling," said Edgar.

"Choose a nice orphan for us to adopt, dear," said Shirley. "Pick up two, if they're not too bulky. I don't care for bulky children."

"I'll see what they have, my pet."

Edgar slid the van door shut, walked up a flight of steep stone stairs to the Jolly Days front door, and rang the bell.

Hortense Jolly opened the door. The smell of

strong hospital soap and something rotten drifted out from behind her.

"Here to look over the new crop?" asked Hortense Jolly with a smile.

"Yes, thanks," said Edgar. "I'm Professor Edgar Spydelle. We spoke by phone."

"Oh yes, Professor. I thought you were bringing *Mrs.* Spydelle."

"Quite right," said Edgar. "And that was something I thought we might discuss."

"Is there a problem?"

"In a way, perhaps. You see, Miss Jolly, my dear wife, Shirley, and I are eager to adopt some orphans. We have a lovely home in a picturesque wooded area, and we have a comfortable income to support an orphan or two, but the fact of the matter is, my wife happens to be . . . How shall I put this?"

"Your wife happens to be *what*, Professor?"

"She happens to be . . . well, a giant spider."

"A giant *spider*, you say?"

"Yes."

"Oh heck, is *that* all?" said Hortense. "I thought it was something *serious.* Professor Spydelle, I have personally placed *many* of my orphans with adopters who are giant bugs. In fact—how's this for coincidence?—I placed two of my kids with giant bugs just the other day."

"My word, you can't be serious!"

"If I'm lying, may I be dipped in boiling oil," said Hortense. "Come on in now and meet the kids.

Hortense Jolly had all the orphans come into the viewing room and line up to meet Edgar. The professor removed a tiny black notebook from his shirt pocket and prepared to take notes.

"Children, this is Professor Spydelle," said Hortense. "He and his wife are interested in adopting an orphan. When I call your name, please step out of line, smile at Professor Spydelle, and take a little bow. Rocco?"

Rocco, the fat bully, aged twelve, stepped out of line and bowed.

"This is Rocco," said Hortense. "I'm proud to

say he no longer wets the bed. If you don't have a bed, he'll sleep on a pile of old rags. He still has all his own teeth. He weighs over two hundred pounds, so he does need quite a lot of food, but he'll eat things you were going to throw out anyway, like month-old milk that's gone cheesy or fish that's green and fuzzy. Thank you, Rocco."

Rocco stepped back in line.

"Orville?"

Orville, a very small boy with dark circles under his eyes, stepped out and bowed. He was seven. He smelled a little like a skunk, only not as good.

"This is Orville," said Hortense. "His teeth are a bit soft, but he can still eat any kind of pudding, or bread if it's wet. He doesn't mind taking out the garbage, and he often finds interesting things in it which he's learned to make into bracelets and other jewelry. Thank you, Orville."

Orville stepped back in line.

"Rosie?"

A girl stepped out of line. She was ten. She had tight blond curls, and cheeks so red, the color might have been painted on.

"This is Rosie," said Hortense. "She can sing 'Old MacDonald Had a Farm' in Polish, complete with moos and oinks. Did you know that *oink-oink* in Polish is *onk-onk*? Well, it is. She can also recite the Pledge of Allegiance in Polish. As a matter of fact, Rosie speaks mainly Polish. Thank you, Rosie."

Rosie didn't move.

"*Dziekuje,* Rosie," said Hortense.

"*Onk-onk,*" said Rosie. She stepped back in line.

"Ellie Mae?"

Another girl stepped out of line. She was eleven and wore a dress made out of a worn-out laundry bag.

"This is Ellie Mae," said Hortense. "She can drive a truck and make Popsicles in a freezer tray. She can also run very fast if it's downhill and you give her a little push. The doctor says most of those sores will probably heal. Thank you, Ellie Mae."

Ellie Mae stepped back in line.

"Wayne?"

Wayne, a big boy with a crazed smile on his face, stepped out of line. He was twelve.

"This is Wayne," said Hortense. "He has definitely stopped setting fires. We're so proud of the way Wayne gets along with the other children since the accident. He never steals, or if he does, he gives whatever he's taken right back."

Wayne grabbed Professor Spydelle's hand as if to shake it, then stole his watch.

"All right, Wayne," said Hortense. "Now give it back."

Wayne stuck out his tongue, then gave back the professor's watch.

"See how nicely he gave it back?" said Hortense. "Good *boy*! Thank you, Wayne."

Wayne stepped back in line.

Hortense introduced thirty-one more orphans. One of them told a joke about a giraffe and a cannibal in a Miami Beach hotel. One of them recited a poem about asparagus. One of them burped all the state capitals in alphabetical order.

When everyone was done, Professor Spydelle seemed befuddled.

"So what do you think, Professor?" asked Hortense. "Which one would you like to adopt?"

"My word, I don't know," said the professor. "I feel a bit overwhelmed."

"There's certainly a lot of talent here," said Hortense proudly.

"I'd like to return home and discuss this with my wife," said the professor.

"Good idea," said Hortense. "I should tell you that a record number of adopters were here earlier today, and most of the children are being considered for adoption. *Seriously* considered. Now, I don't want to put any pressure on you, but I'm expecting to hear from all adopters by five o'clock. Of course, if you make your selection earlier, you'll have a much better chance of getting your first or second choice."

This was something of an exaggeration. Only two adopters had come before the professor, and both had left in disgust after meeting Rocco and Wayne.

"We'll try to come to a speedy decision," said the professor.

CHAPTER 14

Out of the Swamps and into the Sink

After slogging through mud, muck, and rotting vegetation for another hour, looking nervously over their shoulders to see if either the zombie or the Onts were still chasing them, Wally and Cheyenne finally found a clearing in the distance.

Shortly after that, they staggered out of the swamps and stood on solid ground. Their feet still squished in their shoes. They had been lost for five whole days.

"I can't believe we got out of there alive," said Wally. "I can't believe how hungry I am."

"I can't believe I see a diner," said Cheyenne.

"What?" said Wally.

Cheyenne pointed.

About fifty yards ahead of them was an old railroad caboose that had been made into a restaurant. The sputtering neon sign above it read: MA & PA'S EDGE-O'-THE-SWAMPS DINER.

At first they thought it was a mirage, but it was real. The Shluffmuffin twins dragged themselves to the old caboose and staggered inside.

There was the heady smell of frying food. There was the pleasant sound of bacon grease popping and spitting on the griddle. There was a long aisle. On one side of the aisle was a counter with several stools. On the other was a line of booths upholstered in perky blue and yellow vinyl.

The waitresses and the customers stopped eating and stared at Wally and Cheyenne as if they had arrived from another planet.

"Just got out of the swamps," said Cheyenne cheerfully. "That's why we're so filthy and smell so bad. It's great to be back on solid ground, though."

The waitresses and the diners continued to stare at them.

"Been eating bugs and caterpillars for days," said Wally with a fake chuckle. "We sure hope you have something tastier than that on the menu here."

The diners continued to stare, but one of the waitresses came over to them with a welcoming smile.

"You poor darlings," she said. "Why don't y'all sit down in a booth so we can feed you?"

"Thank you so much," said Cheyenne.

The twins walked to a booth, leaving a trail of slimy footprints.

They sat down on the seats, making squooshy sounds on the vinyl cushions. The waitress came back with a fistful of bent silverware, piles of paper napkins, and illustrated menus laminated in stiff plastic.

"My name's Fern," said the waitress. "Y'all look over these menus for a minute and I'll be back to take your orders."

Wally and Cheyenne opened the menus. They couldn't believe all the things that were listed there. Wally counted 187 different dinners they could order. All of them looked scrumptious.

"Well, there's good news and bad news," said Wally. "The good news is that this is the most food I've ever seen in my life. The bad news is that the total money I have left from our cockroach racing bets is sixty-eight cents."

"I don't have any money at all," said Cheyenne. "But that waitress Fern seemed so nice, Wally. Maybe she'll let us eat for free."

"Oh, right," said Wally.

"Well, we have to eat *something*," said Cheyenne. "I don't really feel like going back into the swamps and turning over rocks to find dinner."

"Neither do I," said Wally. "As tasty as that centipede was."

"Look, why don't we just order some food, eat it, and hope for the best?" said Cheyenne.

"Maybe if we don't order anything good, they won't be as angry when they find out we can't pay for it," said Wally. "Maybe we should just order stale bread crusts and gruel."

The waitress came back with an order pad and a pencil.

"Y'all want to hear the specials?" she asked.

"Sure, Fern," said Cheyenne.

"Okay, hon. Well, today we got the lamb shish kebab with moussaka and stuffed grape leaves. We got the broiled lobster stuffed with crab and scallops. We got the sushi platter with octopus, squid, eel, and sea urchin. We got the Chow Fun noodles with Thousand Fragrance Beef. We got the potato latkes with farfel, kasha, and matzo balls. We got the *escargots de Bourgogne,* which is your hot snails in garlic butter. We got the roasted breast of duck with green peppercorn sauce. We got the filet mignon, which is your little round expensive steaks, wrapped in bacon. We got the classic coq au vin, which is your chicken cooked in red wine. And we got the *Scallopine di Vitello alla Alba,* which is your veal topped with crabmeat, asparagus, and fontina cheese in a light cognac sauce."

94

Wally and Cheyenne looked dazed.

"So that's the specials," said the waitress. "Then we have the regular menu, of course, but I gotta warn you. We got only one whole roast suckling pig left. If the both of you want it, one of you's out of luck. You folks ready, or you need a little more time?"

"I think I'm just going to go with stale bread crusts and gruel," said Wally.

"Yeah, me, too," said Cheyenne.

"Sorry, hon, we're fresh out."

"In that case," said Wally, "I'll have a mushroom-spinach-and-feta-cheese omelet, Belgian waffles with fresh strawberries, french fries swimming in gravy, raisin toast with plenty of butter, and pecan pie topped with coconut ice cream and whipped cream."

Cheyenne gave Wally a questioning look.

"Since they're out of stale bread crusts and gruel," he explained.

"In that case," said Cheyenne, "I'll have what *he's* having."

When the food came, the heady aroma that

drifted up to the twins' nostrils almost made them faint. They stuffed themselves till their bellies stretched tight as drums. When the check came, Wally reached into his pocket and put sixty-eight cents on the table.

"What's that, hon?" asked the waitress.

"All the money we've got," said Wally.

"Sorry, Fern," said Cheyenne.

"You're serious?" asked the waitress.

Wally and Cheyenne nodded.

"We would have told you before," said Cheyenne, "but then we would've had to go back into the swamps and eat bugs."

"Where are your parents?"

"Dead," said Wally. "We're orphans."

"I'm gonna have to go get the bosses, hon," she said. "Don't go nowheres."

"Okay," said Cheyenne.

The waitress left.

"You want to run?" asked Wally.

Cheyenne shook her head.

"If we run, they'll call the cops," she said.

"They'll call the cops even if we *don't* run," said Wally.

"Maybe, maybe not," said Cheyenne.

The waitress returned to the table with two people, a chubby gray-haired man and a chubby gray-haired woman. Ma and Pa. Both of them wore white aprons, white chef's hats, silver-rimmed glasses, and frowns.

"So," said Pa, "you the two kids ate the big dinner, knowin' you couldn't pay?"

Wally and Cheyenne nodded.

"You know that's stealin', don't you?" said Pa.

"Yes, sir," said Wally.

"I hear you're orphans," said Ma.

"Yes, ma'am," said Cheyenne.

"Well," said Pa, "you're gonna have to wash dishes to pay for what you et. Does that sound fair?"

Both twins nodded.

"Okay," said Ma. "You kids go get cleaned up in the restroom. Then we'll put you to work."

CHAPTER 15

A New Home in the Kitchen with Ma and Pa

Wally and Cheyenne did so well at dishwashing—even scouring the big pots and pans with boiling water, ammonia, and steel wool, the way they'd learned at the orphanage—that Ma and Pa were extremely impressed. Then the twins got down on their hands and knees and scrubbed and waxed the linoleum till it shone like a mirror.

"I'm gonna tell you a true thing," said Pa. "If you kids was sixteen, we'd hire you permanent."

"We *are* sixteen," said Wally.

"Go on," said Ma. "You look lots younger."

"We lived in an orphanage where they starved us," said Wally.

"Those devils!" said Pa. "If I met 'em, I'd tell 'em a thing or two."

"You poor, poor things!" said Ma.

"They fed us only stale bread crusts and mucus-like gruel," said Wally, "so we probably don't look any more than ten."

"You don't," said Pa. "That's a fact. You don't look any more than ten. Am I right, Ma?"

"Not any more than ten," Ma agreed. "If that."

"So we've been told," said Wally. "And that's one of the saddest things about living at Jolly Days."

"Well, don't you worry your pretty little heads about lookin' young, son," said Pa. "Here at the Edge-o'-the-Swamps Diner, we don't care *how* young you look, long as you do the work and keep your nose clean."

"I'm sorry," said Cheyenne. "I'll try to do better in the nose department, I promise."

"There, there, darlin'," said Ma, patting her head. "Pa didn't mean nothin' by that. He was just usin' a figure of speech. A colloquialism, you might say."

"Oh," said Cheyenne.

So Ma and Pa hired the Shluffmuffin twins full time. The twins didn't mind the work, and Ma and Pa were lots nicer than Hortense Jolly. Although Wally said she was stupid to even think about it, Cheyenne began to secretly dream that Ma and Pa might someday adopt them.

The twins were happy at the Edge-o'-the-Swamps Diner, but somewhere not so very far from where they happily scoured pots and pans, the zombie was growing restless. He had become weary of dragging himself painfully through the muck. Deep within him was a powerful urge to migrate to new painful dragging grounds.

So the zombie drifted beyond the outermost reaches of the swamps and into the innermost reaches of Dripping Fang Forest. Birds in the forest saw him and stopped their twittering. Wolves saw him and trotted off whimpering, their tails between their legs.

Then, in the kitchen one day, the twins saw their photos on a milk carton, and they knew their time was running out.

CHAPTER 16

Run, Shluffmuffins, Run!

One bright Monday morning, a morning so bright that the glare off the whites of the sunny-side-up eggs made you squint, two policemen swaggered into Ma & Pa's Edge-o'-the-Swamps Diner.

Officers Kafka and Beckett had scarcely dipped doughnuts into coffee when they looked again at the two kids who'd brought them their piles of paper napkins and bent silverware.

"Aren't those the two kids we been seein' on the milk cartons?" whispered Beckett as the twins returned to the kitchen.

"The runaways?"

"Yeah," said Beckett. "Wait, I got the carton right here."

He took a folded milk carton out of his pocket, unfolded it, and studied the picture. It was definitely the same kids. The two policemen

got up and walked to the door of the kitchen. The smoky smell of bacon sizzling on the griddle made them want to nibble on the doorframe.

"Your names Walter and Cheyenne Shluff-muffin?" Kafka asked the twins.

"No," said Wally, "we're Thor and Brunhilda Finkelplotz."

"Yeah, well, Thor, we got orders to pick you up," said Kafka.

"For what?" asked Wally.

"For being runaways," said Beckett.

"Runaways?" snorted Wally. "That's ridiculous!"

"Run, Shluffmuffins, run!" yelled Ma.

Wally and Cheyenne tore out the back door of Ma and Pa's kitchen so fast, their sneakers left skid marks on the newly waxed floor.

CHAPTER 17

Six Ways That Spiders and Humans Are Surprisingly Alike

The twins slogged through the swamps for at least ten minutes before Officers Kafka and Beckett caught up with them. All four of them were up to their hips in slime, and mosquitoes were whining in their ears.

"What do you want with us?" asked Wally.

"We haven't done anything wrong," said Cheyenne.

"If you haven't done anything wrong, then why are you running?" asked Kafka.

"We run every day," said Wally. "For aerobic exercise."

"Your adoptive parents have reported you as runaways," said Beckett.

"So they survived the quicksand," said Wally. "Too bad."

"We're not adopted," said Cheyenne. "We were taken on a week's free trial from the Jolly Days Orphanage, but we were never adopted."

"Show them the papers," said Kafka.

Beckett smacked a mosquito on his neck, then took some official-looking papers out of an inside pocket.

"See what it says here?" said Beckett. "Dagmar and Hedy Mandible are the true and legal adoptive parents of Walter and Cheyenne Shluffmuffin."

"We never agreed to that," said Wally.

"You're minors under the age of eighteen," said Kafka. "You don't *have* to agree to it."

"Officer," said Cheyenne, "Dagmar and Hedy Mandible are giant ants."

"They may have been your aunts *before*," said Beckett, "but now they're your *parents*."

"You don't understand," said Wally. "What we're telling you is that Dagmar and Hedy Mandible aren't human. They're giant ants with six legs, black claws, wavy antennae coming out of their foreheads, and horrible mouths that look like huge black pliers, only sharper."

Kafka and Beckett looked at each other and rolled their eyes.

"The Mandibles reported that you two stole several items from their household when you ran away," said Kafka.

"That's so not true!" cried Cheyenne.

"The Mandibles reported that you stole laptop computers and PlayStations and expensive Belgian chocolates," said Beckett.

"We didn't take anything from them," said Cheyenne. "And we're not going back."

"We can either take you to the Mandibles," said Kafka, "or we can take you to the police station and book you, in which case you'll go to jail."

"Jail!" both twins yelled in unison. "*Please* take us to jail!"

The policemen laughed. Then they led the twins back through the swamps toward their patrol car. Thinking it was a log, Beckett nearly stepped on an alligator, and Wally had to fall on it and hold its jaws together while everybody got away.

"Thanks, kid," said Beckett. "You may have just saved my life."

"Does that entitle me and my sister to go free?" asked Wally.

"It should," said Kafka. "Unfortunately, it doesn't."

The drive to Dripping Fang Forest took less than an hour. Just before the police car turned off the highway into the forest, the twins once more begged the officers to stop.

"Please don't take us back to the Mandibles," said Wally. "We know they want to kill us. And the forest will be really dangerous for you, too. Terrible things live in there."

"Yeah? Like what?"

"Like ten-foot-long slugs that eat your feet off," said Wally. "Like man-eating wolves that talk to you before they tear your throat out. Like enormous spiders that serve you tea and ginger-snaps."

Kafka laughed. "You got a great imagination, kid," he said. "You oughta be a writer."

Beckett drove the patrol car into the forest, entering right under the sign that read: DRIPPING FANG FOREST. Next to this was a smaller sign that read: PRIVATE PROPERTY. KEEP OUT. THIS MEANS YOU. TRESPASSERS WILL BE . . .

The word PROSECUTED had been crossed out and somebody had written SHOT above it. The word SHOT had been crossed out, and somebody had written TORN APART BY WOLVES above that.

The road into the forest was sandy and narrow, with deep ruts carved into the soft soil by the few vehicles that had ventured inside. The overhanging trees and vines scraped the patrol car like claws and made it seem as though they were driving into a leafy green funnel. Eventually the space they were driving through grew too narrow for the car to fit.

When they'd turned onto the forest road, it was late morning. It was now so dark it seemed like dusk.

"Okay," said Kafka, "this is about as far as we

can travel by car. We'll go the rest of the way on foot. Everybody out of the vehicle."

"You're making a terrible mistake," said Wally.

"Out of the vehicle now, kids," said Kafka, "I *mean* it."

Kafka, Beckett, Wally, and Cheyenne got out of the car.

An icy wind blew up from nowhere. It fluttered the leaves and shook the trees and made the twins shiver. Somewhere a wolf howled.

"You know something?" said Kafka. "It *is* a little creepy in this forest. I got to admit it."

"Just wait," said Wally.

They continued walking on the road, but the vines and bushes grew closer and tighter together. Then a branch sprang free and whacked Kafka in the back, causing him to tumble to his knees. Beckett got his ankle tangled in a vine, and when he bent down to free himself, his other foot got tangled up, too.

"Lieutenant," said Beckett, "could you please give me a hand here?"

"Just a second," said Kafka. "My foot's caught in brambles or vines or something."

It didn't seem possible, but thick, thorny vines were now growing around the ankles of both policemen. You could actually see the vines growing. If you listened, you could hear tiny creaking sounds as they got longer.

"Please, Lieutenant," said Beckett. "I really need your help here. I'm stuck."

"So am I," said Kafka.

"Pssst!" said a voice in the bushes behind them.

"Did you hear that?" whispered Cheyenne.

"It came from in back of us," said Wally.

"Pssst! Children! Over here," hissed the voice in the bushes.

"It's probably a wolf," said Wally. "I don't want to have any more conversations with wolves."

"It's me, kids," said the voice. "Edgar Spydelle."

"Oh, great," said Wally. "The giant spider's husband."

"Duck down and walk back this way," whispered the voice. "The policemen are too busy to notice."

"What do you want to do?" whispered Wally to his sister. "Stay with the cops and go back to the Onts who'll kill us? Or go home with Edgar and get eaten by a giant spider?"

"I sort of liked old Edgar," said Cheyenne. "He seemed kind."

"Okay," said Wally, "whatever."

The twins ducked down and scurried into the bushes and toward the sound of Edgar's voice.

"Hey!" called Kafka. "Where the heck do you think *you're* going? You kids better get back here!"

"You kids get back here this second or you'll be in real trouble!" called Beckett.

"We couldn't be in more trouble than we are already," called Wally. "Neither could you. Better forget about us and start saving *yourselves.*"

The twins reached Edgar.

"Hello, children," said the professor. "How

lovely to see you again. Shirley will be delighted as well."

"Hi, Professor," said Cheyenne.

"Professor," said Wally, "is there any chance you could help us get out of the forest instead of taking us back to your house?"

"Oh, do you have someplace to stay in Cincinnati?"

"Not really, but . . ."

"Shirley loves children," said Edgar. "In fact, we nearly adopted some orphans from Jolly Days just the other day, but the ones we saw there just weren't . . . quite what we were looking for."

"Professor," said Wally, "can I tell you something, even thought it might hurt your feelings?"

"Why, certainly, Wally. What is it?"

"We don't want to go home with you to see Shirley," said Wally.

"We're afraid of giant insects," said Cheyenne.

"My dear girl," said Edgar with a chuckle. "Spiders aren't insects, they're *arachnids*. There's quite a difference, you know. Arachnids have *eight* legs, insects only six. Insects have three-segmented bodies, whereas arachnids have—"

"Yeah, yeah, I know all that," said Wally, "but the thing is, we just don't get along well with ladies who have lots of legs, all right?"

"Shirley's really quite lovely when you get to know her," said Edgar. "She wouldn't hurt a fly. Okay, that was a poor example—she *snacks* on flies. But I assure you, she wouldn't dream of hurting *you*."

"If only we could be certain of that," said Cheyenne.

A sudden noise in the woods startled the twins.

"What was that?" Cheyenne whispered to her brother.

"It wasn't coming from the cops' direction," whispered Wally.

They listened. There it was again. An eerie sound: *Ch-ch-ch-ch-ch* . . .

"The larvae?" whispered Wally. "You think the larvae somehow crawled out of the basement and got into the woods?"

"I didn't think larvae could crawl," said Cheyenne aloud.

"Larvae *can't* crawl," Edgar agreed. "What sort of larvae are we speaking about, by the way?"

They heard the sound again: *Ch-ch-ch-ch-ch* . . .

Then they smelled a familiar odor.

"Do you smell chocolate?" asked Wally.

Cheyenne sniffed the air. "It's chocolate, all right," she said. She shuddered. "I never thought the smell of chocolate would give me the creeps."

"I'll tell you what," said Edgar. "Come home with me, but stay outside and chat with Shirley through the open door. If she still scares you, I will personally escort you out of the forest."

"I'm willing to try it," said Cheyenne. "What about you, Wally?"

"Let's do it," said Wally.

So the twins went back to the Spydelles' house and had a nice chat with Shirley at a safe distance. They found her unexpectedly pleasant. She seemed quite sympathetic about their

115

problems with the Onts. She even had a sense of humor. The twins hadn't known that giant spiders could be funny.

At last they agreed to go inside. It took a real effort to get comfortable with her eight eyes and her eight hairy legs, but once they did, Shirley was really a blast to talk to. She didn't try to pretend she was normal looking. She made jokes about her many eyes and legs. She told them stories—one about going to the Cincinnati Department of Motor Vehicles to get a driver's license and another about going to a department store to buy pantyhose—that were so hilarious, the twins almost wet their pants. In fact, they liked Shirley so much, they agreed to stay a few days.

That night Cheyenne sat by the fireplace, writing. Once or twice she stopped and listened. She thought she heard a sound outside in the woods: *Ch-ch-ch-ch-ch* ... Once she thought she smelled the odor of chocolate drifting in through an open window.

"What are you writing there, Cheyenne?" asked Wally.

Cheyenne showed him:

A List of Ways That Spiders and Humans Are Surprisingly Alike

1. Both have more than one leg.
2. Both have at least two eyes.
3. Both love dark cozy places.
4. Both love children.
5. Both have a great sense of humor.
6. Both enjoy jumping out of hiding places and biting strangers (mainly true of spiders).

CHAPTER 18

Showdown at the Spydelles'

The sun had just set, but Dripping Fang Forest was already long shrouded in gloom and darkness. The insects of the night had begun their noisy chatter. The fragrance of the forest was of moist earth and rotting vegetation.

Shuffling through the forest, the zombie had seen the twins enter the Spydelles' house. He lurked in the bushes, waiting for a chance to confront them.

Two hours later, when Cheyenne and Wally left the house briefly to bring in some firewood, a stranger in a black trench coat hurried over.

"Hello, frightfully sorry to bother you," said the stranger, "but I'm afraid I'm a bit lost. Would

you happen to know where I might find the Thorsten Veblen home?"

"I'm afraid I can't help you," said Cheyenne. "I don't know this forest at all."

Wally thought the stranger's raspy voice sounded familiar.

"Cheyenne, you know who this guy sounds like?" whispered Wally.

"Who?" whispered Cheyenne.

"Fred," whispered Wally.

"Fred? Who's Fred?" whispered Cheyenne.

"Fred, the leader of the wolf pack," said the stranger. He grabbed Cheyenne's sleeve in his teeth.

Both Shluffmuffins screamed.

Close by, the zombie's rotting mind flashed images from his prezombie life: A playground with small children on swings and teeter-totters. A roller coaster crammed full of kids screaming with laughter. A circus . . . a high-wire act . . . trapeze artists . . . fifteen clowns tumbling out of a tiny Volkswagen . . . elephants in little pink ballet skirts . . . a bear riding a bicycle . . . a Porta

Potti . . . then falling in slow motion and sinking into total darkness.

The zombie lurched out of hiding. He looked awful and smelled worse. The wolf leader took one look at the zombie and bolted, whimpering.

The twins retreated from the zombie in horror. As they scrambled back into the house, the zombie spoke. "Shy! Wa! Me Da!"

Cheyenne was just about to slam the door when the zombie began to sing.

"Issy bissy spy clyde uppa waaa spow," he sang. "Lon cayma rayna washa spy ow."

Cheyenne's eyes opened so wide, her eyeballs nearly fell out of their sockets.

"Do you hear what that thing is singing?" she whispered to her brother.

"You think it's *singing*?" Wally asked.

"Yes, listen," said Cheyenne. "It's singing, 'Itsy bitsy spider climbed up the waterspout.'"

"That's what *Dad* used to sing to us when he put us to sleep," said Wally.

"Dad?" called Cheyenne through the door. She was horrified.

"Dad, is that *you*?" called Wally, already sick to his stomach at the thought.

"Shy, Wa!" shouted the zombie. "Shy, Wa! Me Da!"

It was incredible. Could this disgusting zombie really be their father, Sheldon Shluffmuffin, who had drowned three years before in a Porta Potti at the circus? The thought filled them with a mix of powerful emotions.

They loved their father and missed him achingly, but if this was really him, in the past three years he had changed quite a bit.

Wally came cautiously out of the house to take a closer look. From somewhere came a familiar sound. *Ch-ch-ch-ch-ch* ... From somewhere came the unmistakable smell of chocolate.

Hedy and Dagmar Mandible crept through the dense foliage, moving toward the Spydelle house.

"I hear the children's voices," said Dagmar. "Get ready to strike the instant I give the signal."

"I'm ready, dearest," whispered Hedy. "We

122

shall show them no mercy. Unless, of course, you think mercy might be a good idea . . ."

"No mercy," snapped Dagmar. They were almost up to the Spydelle house.

"Shy, Wa, me Da," mumbled the zombie, which could have meant "Cheyenne, Wally, I'm your dad."

Hedy and Dagmar came around the corner of the Spydelle house and caught sight of the zombie for the first time. They stared at him in horrified fascination.

"Hmm," said Hedy.

"Hmm," said Dagmar.

"I was thinking," whispered Hedy. "This might not be the absolute best time to strike after all."

"You may be right," said Dagmar. She stared through the bushes at the zombie. "No, you're *definitely* right about this. You don't want to be striking orphans without mercy and then have some zombie mess up your timing." She switched to her hollow, echoey voice: "We may be leaving now, Shluffmuffins, but make no mistake—we shall return."

Dagmar and Hedy retreated into the darkness.

"Oh boy," said Wally, coming as close to the zombie as he dared, looking hard and trying not to vomit. "Oh boy. Well, sis, there's semi-good news and there's really disappointing news."

"What's the semi-good news?" asked Cheyenne hopefully.

"The semi-good news is, I think this zombie *is* our dad," said Wally.

"And what's the really disappointing news?"

"The really disappointing news is, zombies are the walking dead, so . . ."

". . . so, technically, we're still orphans," said Cheyenne sadly.

"Right," said Wally.

What's Next for the Shluffmuffin Twins?

Will Wally and Cheyenne let Edgar and Shirley adopt them? What would it be like to have an enormous spider for a mom?

What will happen to poor Zombie Dad? How hard is it to have a meaningful relationship with your father when he's dead and losing body parts all over the place?

What did Dagmar mean when she said: "We may be leaving now, Shluffmuffins, but make no mistake—we shall return"? In what hideous and disgusting way do you think she and Hedy will *next* contact the twins?

You seriously can*not* afford to miss the Shluff-muffins' next blood-curdling, gut-wrenching, nausea-inducing adventure—Secrets of Dripping Fang, Book Three: *The Vampire's Curse*!

DAN GREENBURG writes the popular Zack Files series for kids and has also written many bestselling books for grown-ups. His sixty-six books have been translated into twenty languages. To research his writing, Dan has worked with N.Y. firefighters and homicide cops, searched for the Loch Ness monster, flown upside down in an open-cockpit plane, taken part in voodoo ceremonies in Haiti, and disciplined tigers on a Texas ranch. He has not, however, personally encountered any zombies or glowing slugs—at least not yet. Dan lives north of New York with wife Judith, son Zack, and many cats.

SCOTT M. FISCHER glided through high school doing extra-credit art assignments for math teachers, which is kinda boring stuff to draw. Next he went to art school, where he learned to paint even more boring things—like flower vases. However, he swears that since then he has drawn nothing but cool stuff—like oozy, drooling monsters, treacherous villains, and the occasional flower vase . . . that has fangs and eats flowers for breakfast!